Excuse Me

BY JANET RIEHECKY

Published by The Child's World®
1980 Lookout Drive • Mankato, MN 56003-1705
800-599-READ • www.childsworld.com

ISBN 9781503855762 (Reinforced Library Binding)
ISBN 9781503856189 (Portable Document Format)
ISBN 9781503856424 (Online Multi-user eBook)
LCCN: 2021940164

Printed in the United States of America

Manners matter all the day through.

Say, "I'm sorry," or "I didn't mean to."

"Please," or "May I," or "After you,"

will help with what you want to do.

When you treat others with respect and care,

you'll find you have friends everywhere!

Say, **"Excuse me,"** when you bump into someone.

Say, "Excuse me," when you need to leave the table.

Say, **"Excuse me,"** when you burp.

Say, **"Excuse me,"** when you need to get past someone.

Say, **"Excuse me,"** when you step on your friend's toe.

Say, **"Excuse me,"**
when you leave your guest alone.

Say, **"Excuse me,"** when you sit in someone else's seat.

Excuse me.
I didn't
mean to.

Say, **"Excuse me,"**
when you squirt ketchup on your sister.

Say, **"Excuse me,"** when you need to interrupt your mother.

Say, **"Excuse me,"** when you want to get your teacher's attention.

Say, **"Excuse me,"** when you reach in front of someone.

Say, **"Excuse me,"** when you need to walk between two people.

Say, **"Excuse me,"** when you walk into the wrong room.

Say, **"Excuse me,"** when you want to get someone's attention or make an apology.

Activities

Explain to an adult:
After reading this book, explain to an adult why people say, "Excuse me." There are many different reasons!

Act it out:
Use one or more of the examples from this book. Act it out with a friend. You can take turns being the person who must say, "Excuse me."

Word List

apology
attention
interrupt
manners
respect

About the Author

Janet Riehecky is an award-winning author who decided to become a writer when she was ten years old. She has written more than 120 books for young readers. Janet lives in Illinois.